***All children have a great ambition to read to themselves**... and a sense of achievement when they can do so.*

The **read it yourself** *series has been devised to satisfy their ambition. Even before children begin to learn to read formally, perhaps using a reading scheme, it is important that they have books and stories which will actively encourage the development of essential pre-reading skills. Books at Level 1 in this series have been devised with this in mind and will supplement pre-reading books available in any reading scheme.*

Children need to develop left to right eye movements and to perceive differences in word and letter shapes. Based on well-known nursery rhymes and games which children will have heard, these simple pre-readers introduce key words and phrases which children will meet in later reading. These are repeated and the full-colour artwork provides picture clues for new words.

Many young children will remember the words rather than read them but this is a normal part of pre-reading. It is recommended that the parent or teacher should read the book aloud to the child first and then go through the story, with the child reading the text.

British Library Cataloguing in Publication Data

Murdock, Hy

The house that Jack built.—(Read it yourself. Level 1).
1. Readers—1950-
I. Title II. Oakley, Pat III. Series
428.6 PE1119

ISBN 0-7214-0963-6

First edition

Published by Ladybird Books Ltd Loughborough Leicestershire UK
Ladybird Books Inc Auburn Maine 04210 USA

Printed in England

The house that Jack built

devised by Hy Murdock
illustrated by Pat Oakley
of Hurlston Design Ltd

Ladybird Books

This is the house that Jack built.

This is the house.

This is the malt,
That lay in the house
that Jack built.

This is the malt.

This is the rat,
That ate the malt,
That lay in the house
that Jack built.

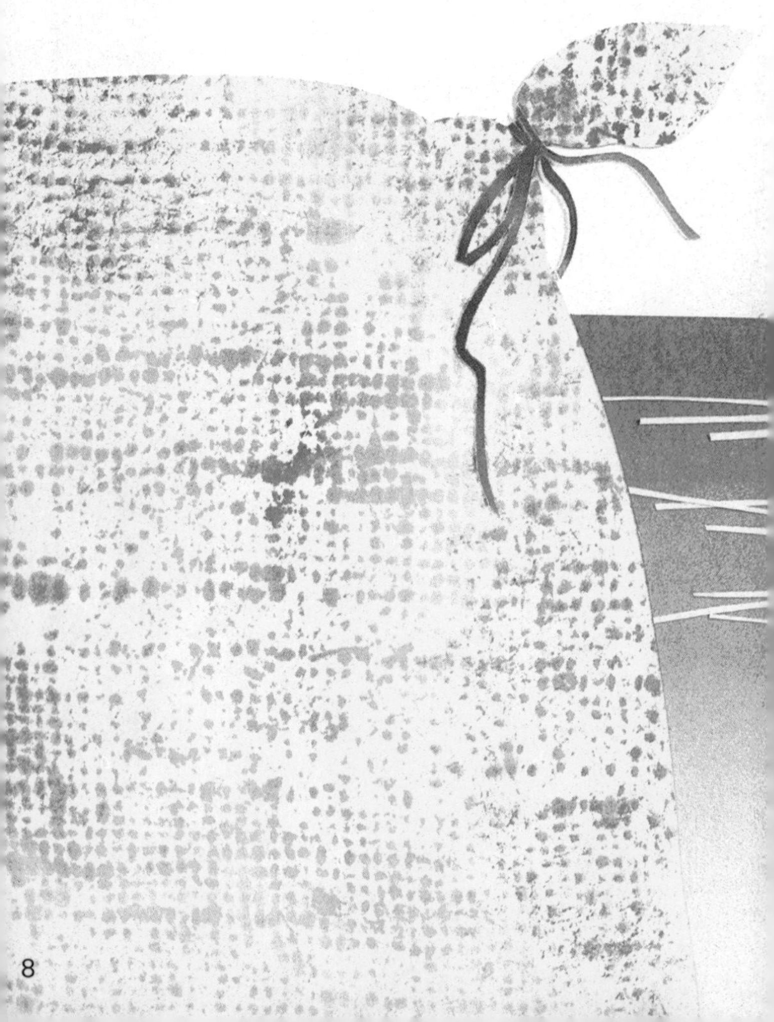

This is the rat.

The rat ate the malt.

TAUGHT

TAUGHT

This is the cat,
That killed the rat,
That ate the malt,
That lay in the house
that Jack built.

This is the cat.

The cat killed the rat.

This is the dog,
That worried the cat,
That killed the rat,
That ate the malt,
That lay in the house
that Jack built.

This is the dog.

The dog worried the cat.

This is the cow
with the crumpled horn,
That tossed the dog,
That worried the cat,
That killed the rat,
That ate the malt,
That lay in the house
that Jack built.

This is the cow.

The cow tossed
the dog.

This is the maiden all forlorn,
That milked the cow
with the crumpled horn,
That tossed the dog,
That worried the cat,
That killed the rat,
That ate the malt,
That lay in the house
that Jack built.

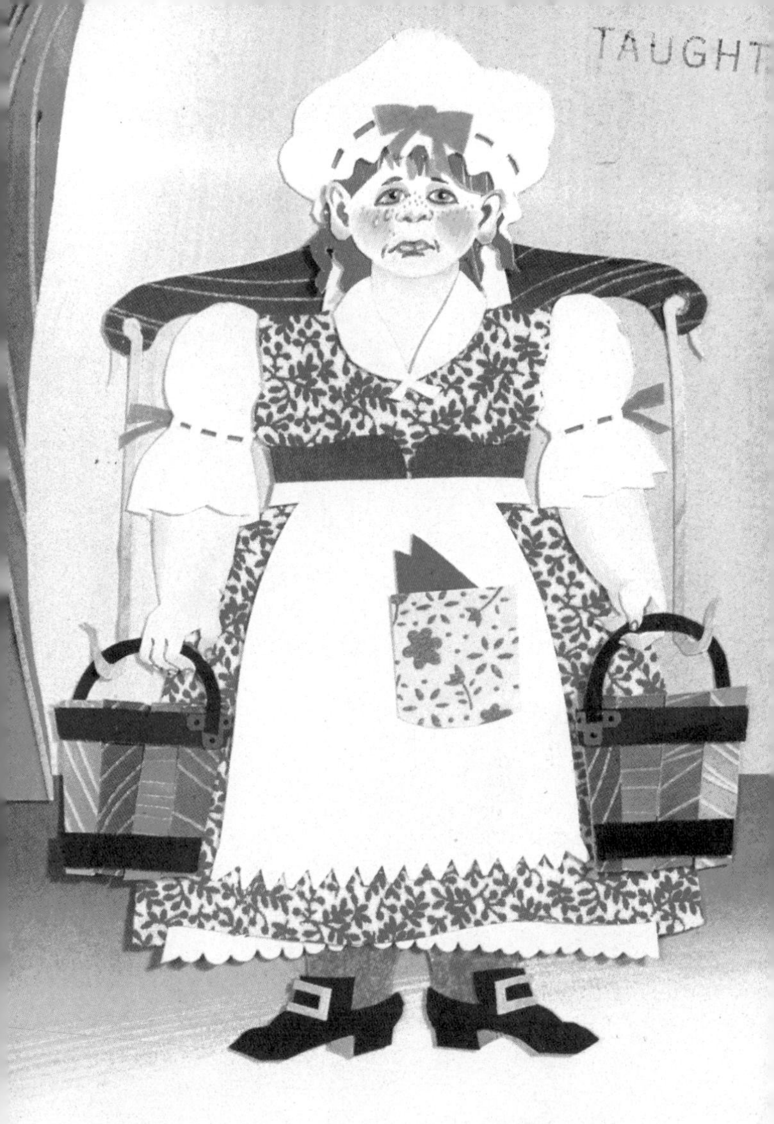

This is the maiden.

The maiden milked
the cow.

This is the man
all tattered and torn,
That kissed the maiden
all forlorn,
That milked the cow
with the crumpled horn,
That tossed the dog,
That worried the cat,
That killed the rat,
That ate the malt,
That lay in the house
that Jack built.

This is the man.

The man kissed the maiden.

This is the priest
all shaven and shorn,
That married the man
all tattered and torn,
That kissed the maiden
all forlorn,
That milked the cow
with the crumpled horn,
That tossed the dog,
That worried the cat,
That killed the rat,
That ate the malt,
That lay in the house
that Jack built.

This is the priest.

The priest married the man and the maiden.

This is the cock
that crowed in the morn,
That waked the priest
all shaven and shorn,
That married the man
all tattered and torn,
That kissed the maiden
all forlorn,
That milked the cow
with the crumpled horn,
That tossed the dog,
That worried the cat,
That killed the rat,
That ate the malt,
That lay in the house
that Jack built.

This is the cock.

The cock crowed
in the morn.

This is the farmer
sowing his corn,
That kept the cock
that crowed in the morn,
That waked the priest
all shaven and shorn,
That married the man
all tattered and torn,
That kissed the maiden
all forlorn,
That milked the cow
with the crumpled horn,
That tossed the dog,
That worried the cat,
That killed the rat,
That ate the malt,
That lay in the house
that Jack built.

This is the farmer.

Who can you see in this picture?